Go away, Baby!

First published in 2009
by Wayland

This paperback edition published in 2010 by Wayland

Text copyright © Claire Llewellyn
Illustration copyright © Polona Lovšin

Wayland
338 Euston Road
London NW1 3BH

Wayland Australia
Level 17/207 Kent Street
Sydney, NSW 2000

Series Editor: Louise John
Editor: Katie Powell
Cover design: Paul Cherrill
Design: D.R.ink
Consultant: Shirley Bickler

A CIP catalogue record for this book is available from the British Library.

ISBN 9780750259149 (hbk)
ISBN 9780750259323 (pbk)

Printed in China

Wayland is a division of Hachette Children's Books,
an Hachette UK Company

www.hachette.co.uk

Go away, Baby!

Written by Claire Llewellyn
Illustrated by Polona Lovšin

I was playing with
the bricks and
Baby came to play.

5

I was playing with
the farm and
Baby came to play.

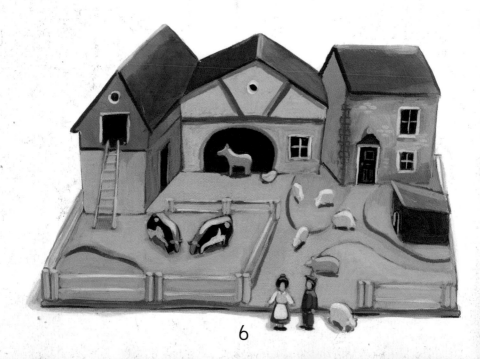

7

I was playing with
the cars and
Baby came to play.

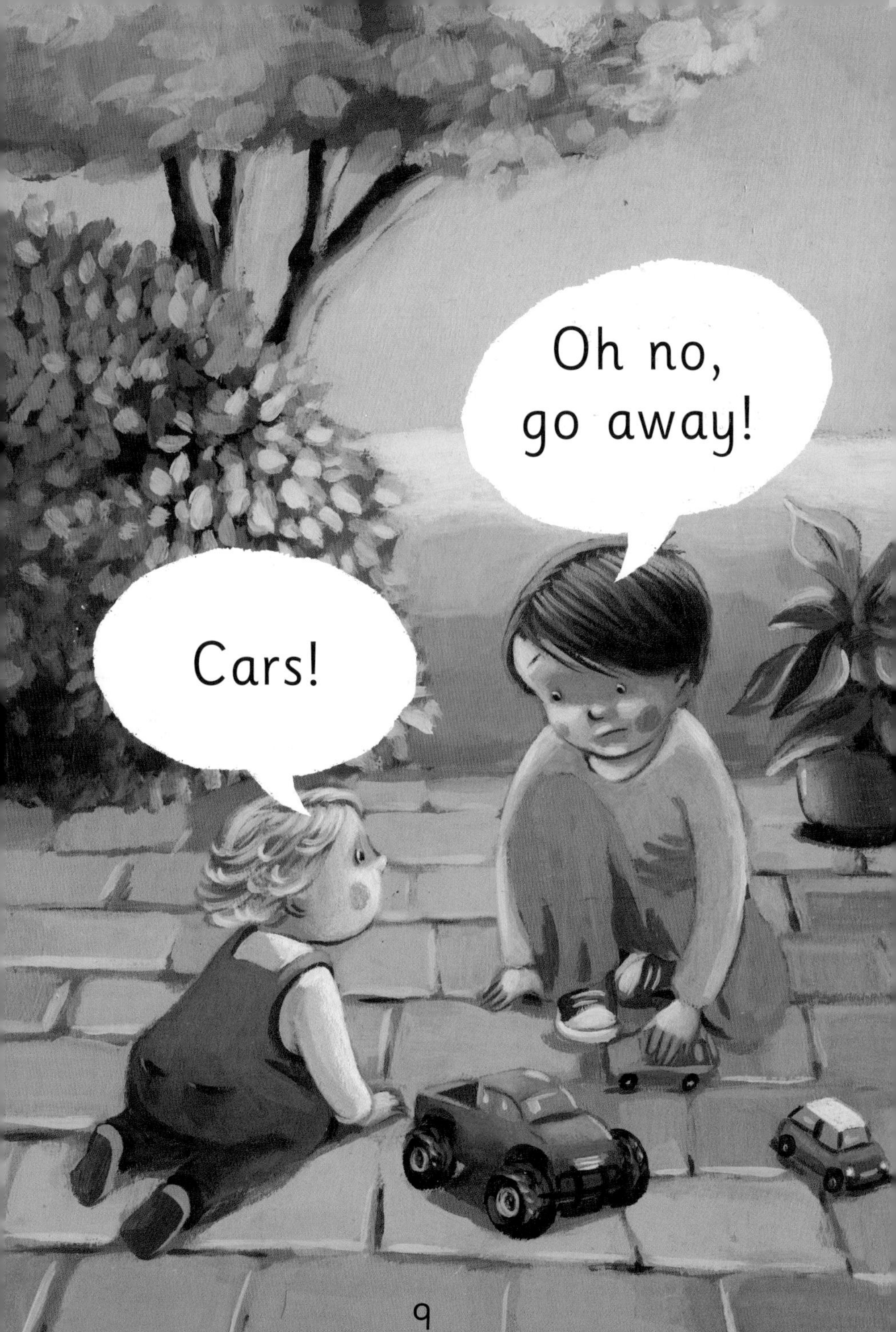
Oh no,
go away!
Cars!

I was playing with Mum
and Baby came to play.

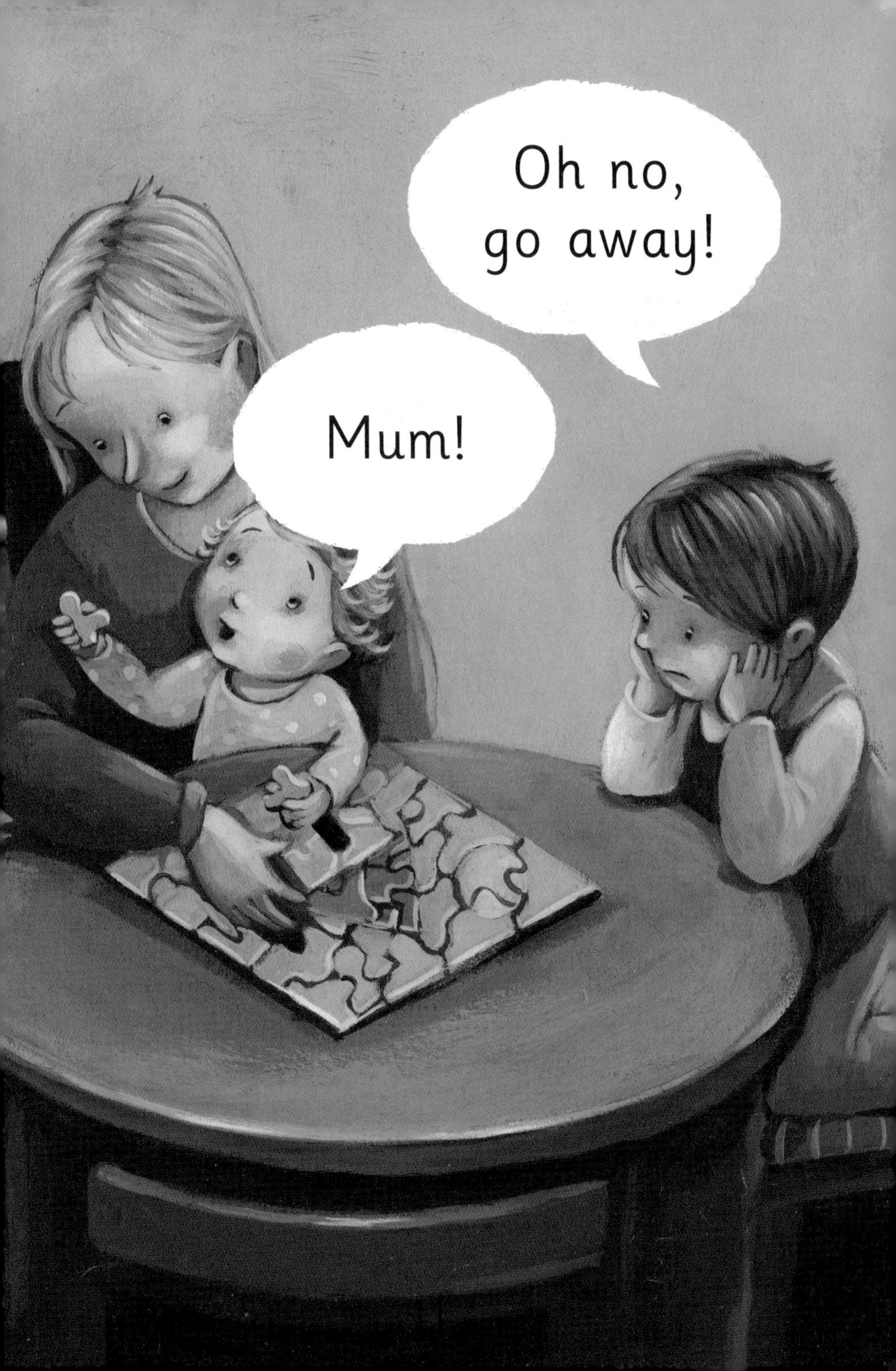
Oh no,
go away!
Mum!

I was playing with
the castle and
Baby came to play.

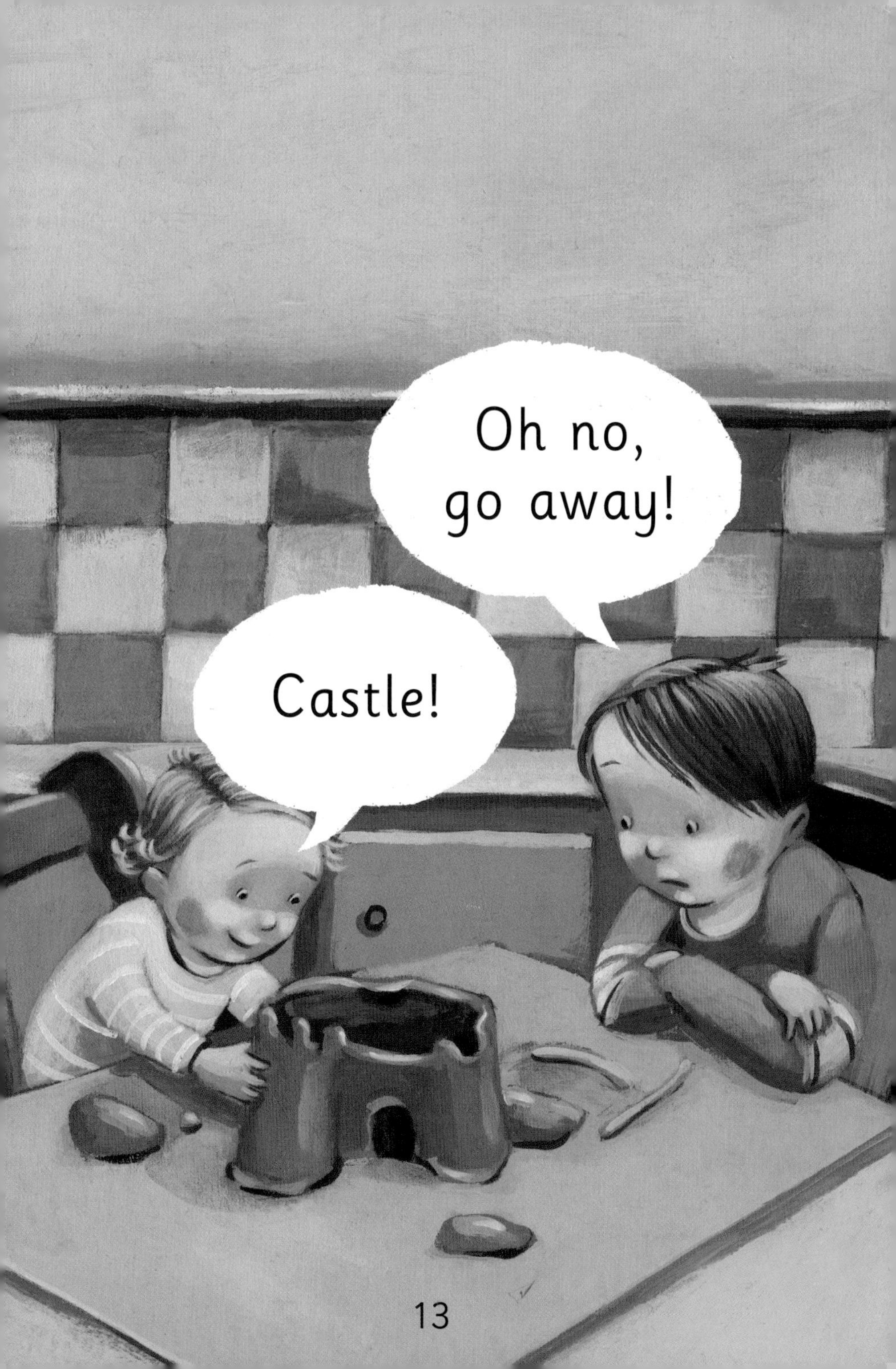
Oh no, go away!
Castle!

I was playing with Dad
and Baby came to play.

15

I was playing with
the paints and
Baby came to play.

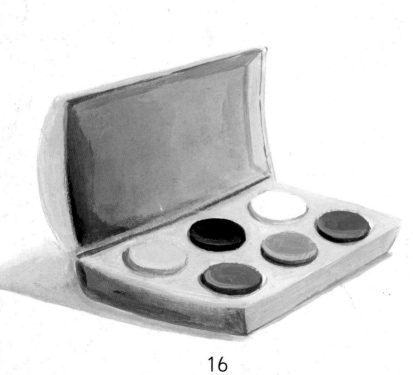

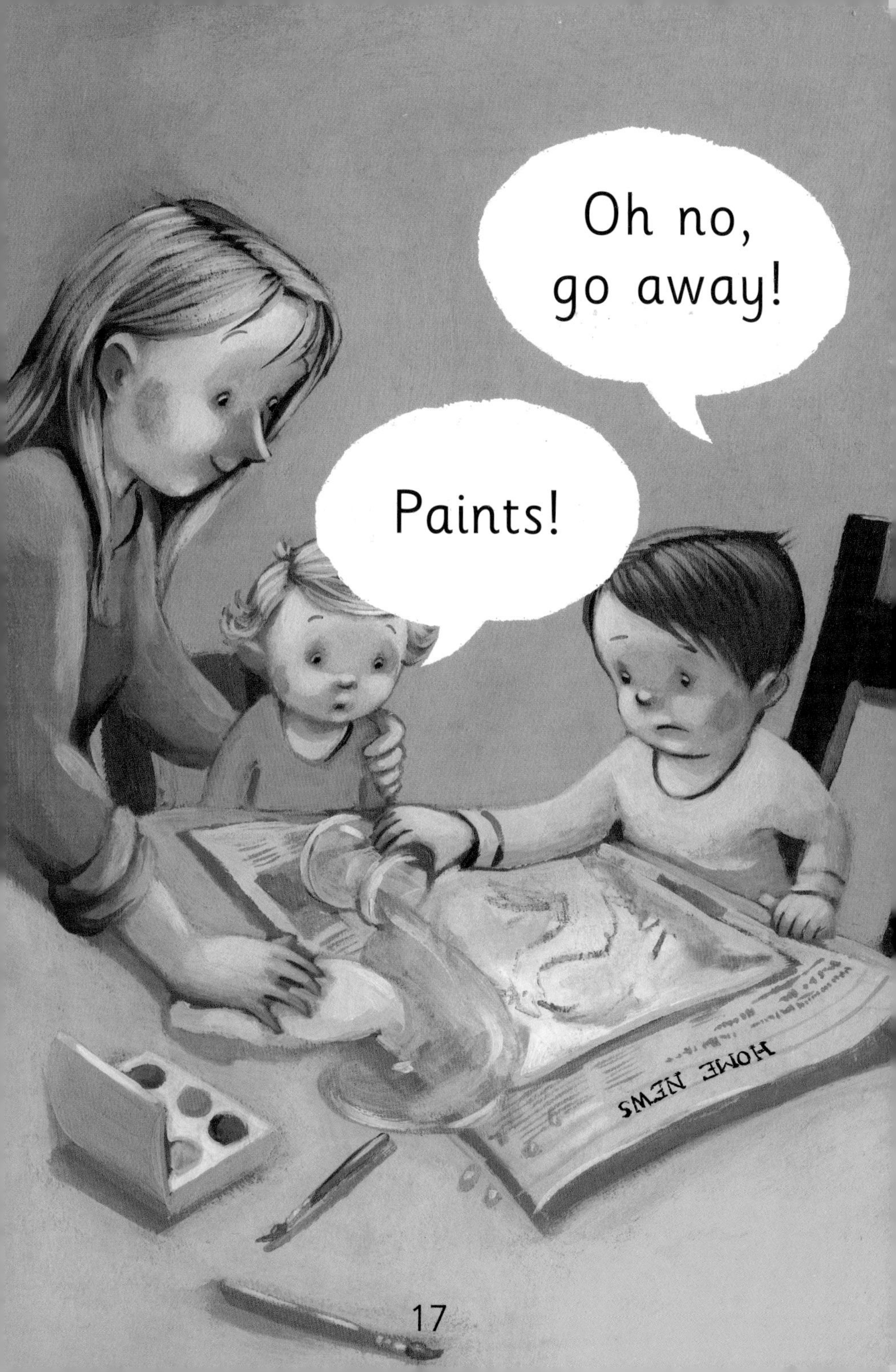
Oh no, go away!
Paints!
HOME NEWS

I was playing with
the boat and
Baby came to play.

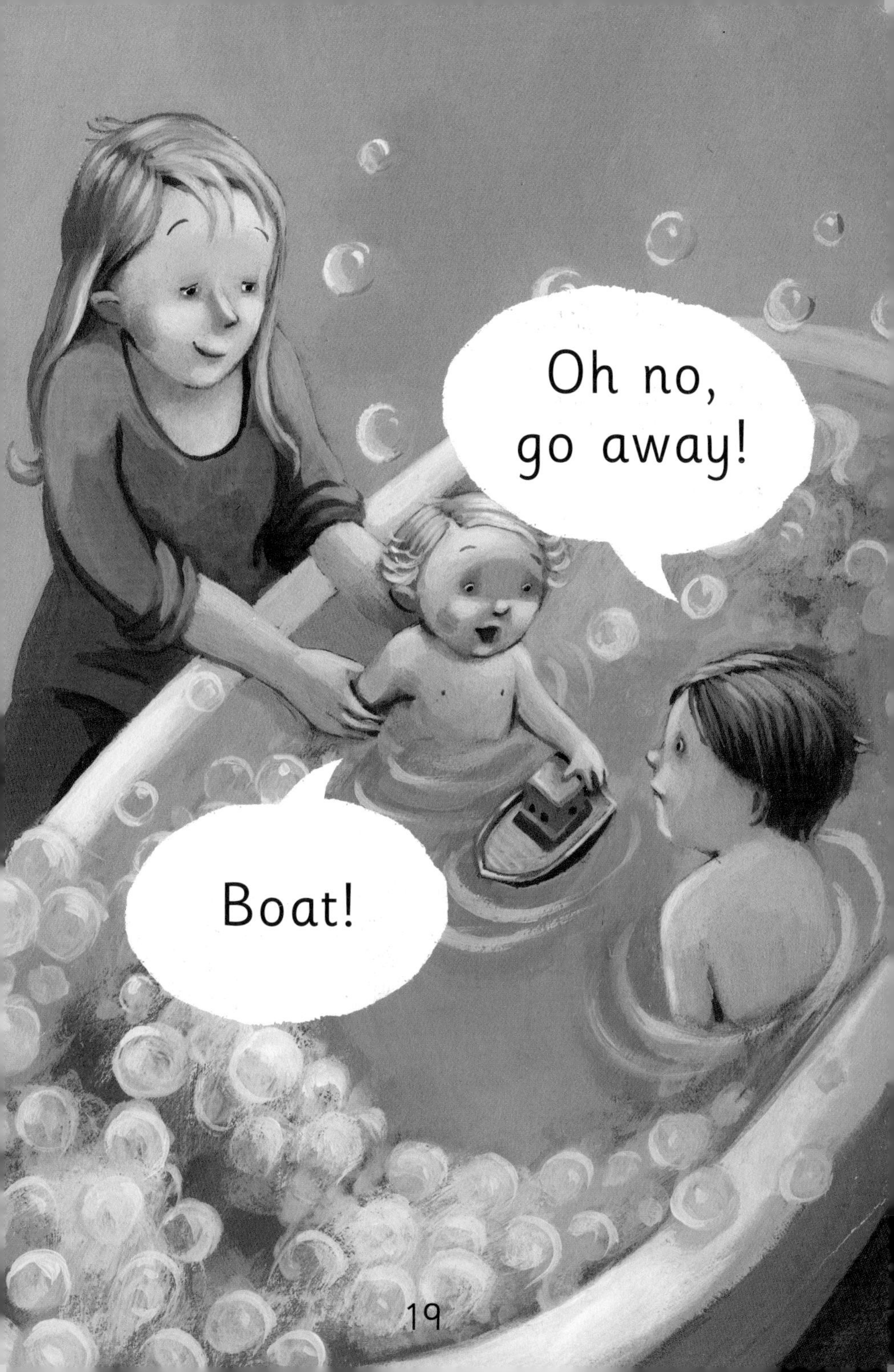
Oh no, go away!
Boat!

I was playing with Baby
and Mum came in.

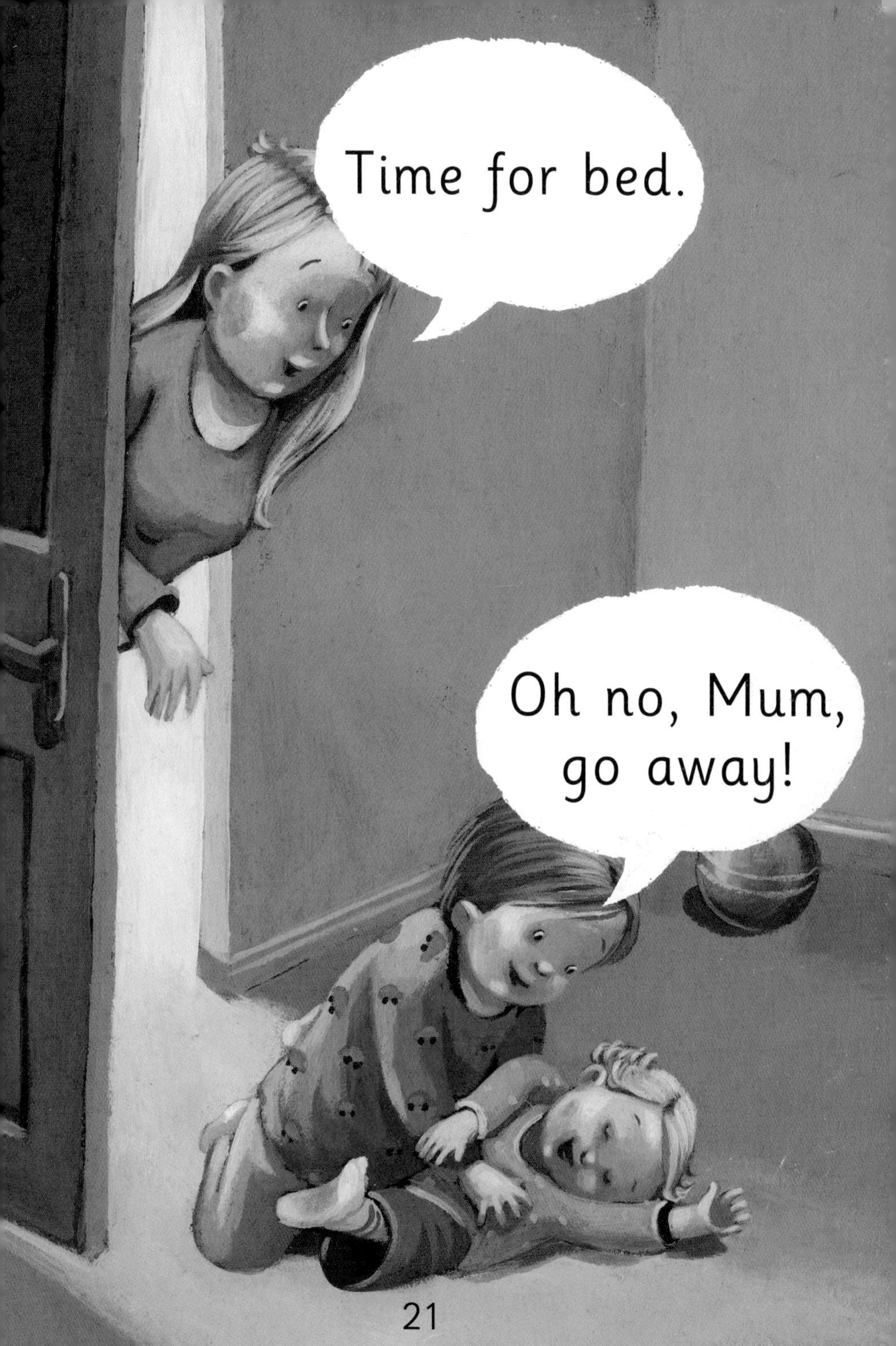
Time for bed.
Oh no, Mum, go away!

Guiding a First Read
Go away, Baby!

It is important to talk through the book with the child before they read it alone. This prepares them for the way the story unfolds, and allows them to enjoy the pictures as you both talk naturally, using the language they will later encounter when reading. Read them the brief overview, and then follow the suggestions below:

The high frequency words in this title are:
go   I   no   play   the   to   was   with

1. Talking through the book

The boy tells us about playing with his toys and how Baby came to play too. "Oh, no, go away!" he said.

Let's read the title: Go away, Baby!
Turn to page 4. The boy said, "I was playing with the bricks and Baby came to play."

Look at the picture on page 5. Here, Baby says, "Bricks!" but the boy is upset.
Why do you think the boy is upset?
What does he say?

Continue to read the book, with the child looking at the illustrations, for example on page 20:

Mum says, "Time for bed," but the boy doesn't want to go to bed. So what does he say? That's right, "Oh no, Mum, go away!"

2. A first reading of the book

Ask the child to read the book independently and point carefully underneath each word (tracking), while thinking about the story.

Work with the child, prompting them and praising their careful tracking, attempts to correct themselves and their knowledge of letters and sounds, for example:

> **I like the way you checked the picture and the first letter of the word to work out what it said. Try that again and think about whether it makes sense.**

3. Follow-up activities

- Select a high frequency word, as listed on p22, and ask the child to find it throughout the book. Discuss the shape of the letters and the letter sounds.

- To memorise the word, ask the child to write it in the air, then write it repeatedly on a whiteboard or on paper, leaving a space between each attempt.

- Alternate writing the new word starting with a capital letter, and then with a lower-case letter.

4. Encourage

- Rereading of the book many times.

- Drawing a picture based on the story.

- Writing a sentence using the practised word.

START READING is a series of highly enjoyable books for beginner readers. **The books have been carefully graded to match the Book Bands widely used in schools.** This enables readers to be sure they choose books that match their own reading ability.

Look out for the Band colour on the book in our Start Reading logo.

The Bands are:

Pink Band 1A and 1B

Red Band 2

Yellow Band 3

Blue Band 4

Green Band 5

Orange Band 6

Turquoise Band 7

Purple Band 8

Gold Band 9

START READING books can be read independently or shared with an adult. They promote the enjoyment of reading through satisfying stories supported by fun illustrations.

Claire Llewellyn has written many books for children. Some of them are about real things like animals and the Moon, others are storybooks. Claire has two children, but they are getting too big for stories like this one. She hopes you will enjoy reading her stories instead.

Polona Lovšin was born in Ljubljana, Slovenia in 1973. She graduated from the Academy of Fine Arts in Ljubljana. Polona loves to draw people, especially children and finds that each new book brings many challenges but lots of fun, too!